Bear Has a Story to Tell

Written by Philip C. Stead   Illustrated by Erin E. Stead

ANDERSEN PRESS

700039896955

For Neal and Jennifer, who listen to our stories

This paperback edition first published in 2012 by Andersen Press Ltd.,
20 Vauxhall Bridge Road, London SW1V 2SA.
First published by Roaring Brook Press, a division of Holtzbrinck Publishing
Holdings Limited Partnership.
Published by arrangement with Rights People, London.

Printed and bound in Singapore by Tien Wah Press.

10   9   8   7   6   5   4   3   2   1

British Library Cataloguing in Publication Data available.

ISBN 978 1 84939 518 2

This book has been printed on acid-free paper

It was almost winter and Bear was getting sleepy.

But first, Bear had a story to tell.

"Mouse, would you like to hear a story?" asked Bear with a yawn.
"I am sorry, Bear," said Mouse, "but it is almost winter and I have
  many seeds to gather."

Bear helped Mouse find seeds on the forest floor.

When they had finished, Mouse said, "See you soon!"
and tunnelled underground to wait for spring.

Bear took slow, sleepy steps through the forest. Fallen leaves crunched under his feet.

"Hello, Duck," said Bear, sitting down to rest his tired legs.
"Would you like to hear a story?"
"I am sorry, Bear," said Duck, "but it is almost winter, and I am
getting ready to fly south."

"I will miss you, Duck," said Bear. He raised a paw to check the direction of the wind.

"I will miss you too," said Duck, and off he flew.

The sun was heavy and hung low in the sky. Bear's eyelids were getting heavy too. He counted colours to stay awake. "Three pink clouds, two red leaves, one green . . ."

"Frog! Hello!" said Bear. "Would you like to hear a story?"
"I am sorry, Bear," said Frog, "but it is almost winter, and I have to find a warm place to sleep."

Bear dug a frog-sized hole between two evergreens. Then he tucked Frog in under a blanket of leaves and pine needles. "Thank you, Bear," said Frog. "I will see you in the spring."

Bear leaned against the old oak tree. He stretched, and yawned, and scratched at his belly. "I wonder if Mole is awake?" he thought.

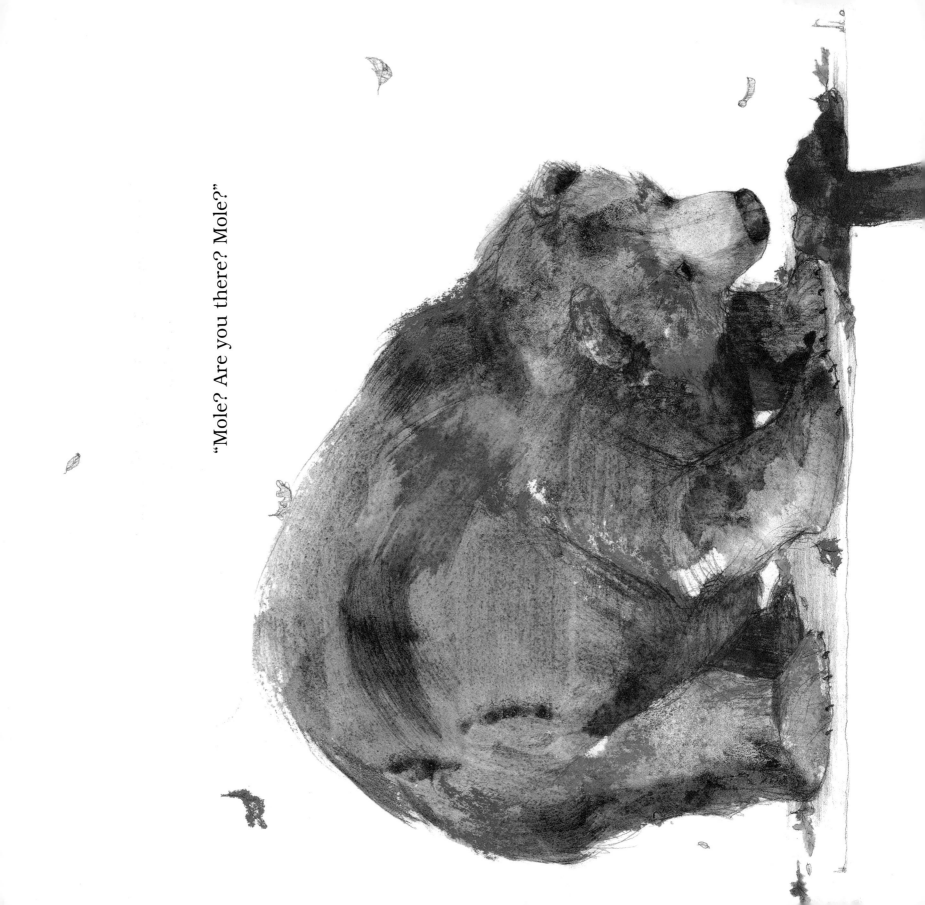

"Mole? Are you there? Mole?"

Mole was already asleep.

"Goodnight, Mole," said Bear with a sigh.

The first winter snowflakes began to fall . . .

Many months passed and the sun returned. It melted the snow and woke the trees. Bear rolled out onto the green grass. "It's spring!" he said. "Now I can tell my story!"

But first, Bear brought Mouse an acorn.
"Thank you, Bear!" said Mouse. Mouse was hungry
after a long winter.

"Welcome home, Duck!" called Bear. "You must be tired from your journey." Bear showed Duck a shady mud puddle he'd found.

Bear placed Frog in the sunshine till he was warm and awake.
Frog opened one eye, then the other.
"Good morning!" said Bear.

Bear, Mouse, Duck, and Frog waited all day for Mole to wake up.
Finally, Mole poked his nose out into the moonlight.
"Mole!" said Bear. "Would you like to hear a story?"

Bear gathered his friends. He sat up straight and cleared his throat.
He puffed out his chest, and with all of his friends listening . . .

Bear could not remember his story. "It was such a good story," he said, hanging his head. "But winter is a very long time for a bear to remember."

The friends sat together for a quiet minute.

Then Mouse said, "Maybe your story is about a bear."
And Duck said, "Maybe your story is about the busy time just
before winter."
"I think there should be other characters too," suggested Frog.
"Like a mole!" said Mole. "And a mouse, and a duck, and a frog!"

Bear sat up straight again. He cleared his throat, puffed out his
chest, and began his story with . . .

"It was almost winter and Bear was getting sleepy."